CONTENTS

NELSON
CENGAGE Learning

Australia • Brazil • Japan • Korea • Mexico • Singapore • Spain • United Kingdom • United States

Everyone Needs Salt

Salt is an important part
of our diet.
It is often in food.

bread

fish

rock salt

peanut butter

cheese

table salt

We need a small amount of salt every day to stay healthy.
But we should not eat too much!

3

PLEASE
KEEP OFF
SALT PONDS

Solar Salt

Solar salt comes
from the sea,
or from salty lakes.

The salty water
is pumped
into special ponds.

Then the sun dries
up the water.
Salt is left behind.

This salt is called
solar salt.

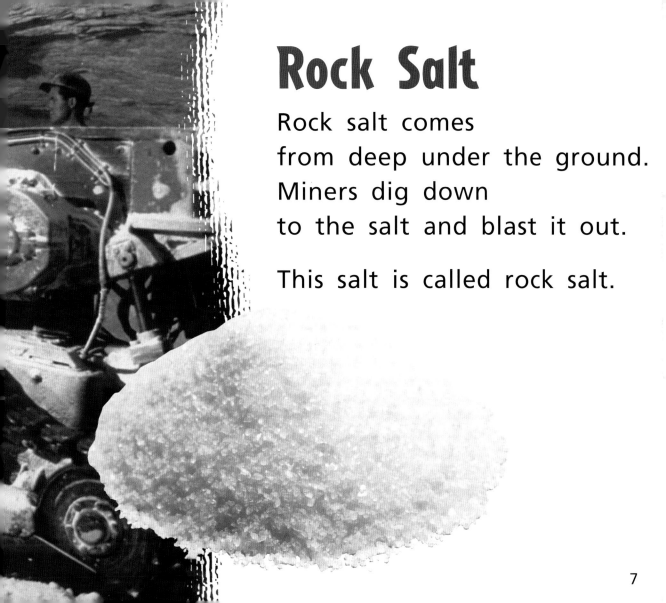

Rock Salt

Rock salt comes
from deep under the ground.
Miners dig down
to the salt and blast it out.

This salt is called rock salt.

Table Salt

Some table salt comes from under the ground, too.

Water and salt are pumped into **wells**, under the ground.

Special machines then take the salt from the water.

Salt Long Ago

Long ago, salt was very **valuable**.
In some places, it was used
instead of money!

Traders sold salt at markets. Sometimes it was swapped for other goods.

Animals and Salt

Animals need salt to stay healthy, too.

Some wild animals look for places
where the ground is salty.
They lick the salty ground.

Some farmers give their animals big blocks of salt to lick. Sometimes farmers add salt to their animals' food.

Did You Know?

When it snows, salt is put
on the paths and roads.
The salt melts
the snow and ice.
It stops the paths and roads
from getting slippery.

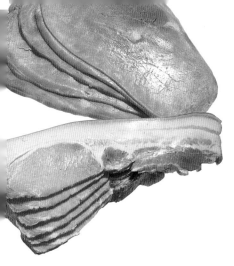

Salt is used
to **preserve** some foods.
It also makes them
taste good!

Salt is made up
of tiny **crystals**.
If you look
at salt through
a microscope,
you will see them!

Glossary

crystals tiny pieces of salt

preserve keep for a long time without going bad

traders people who buy and sell things

valuable worth a lot of money, or of great importance

wells holes that are drilled into the ground to collect things like salt or oil

Index